BUFFALO THUNDER

by **PATRICIA WITTMANN** • *illustrated by* **BERT DODSON**

MARSHALL CAVENDISH

New York

Text copyright © 1997 by Patricia Wittmann • Illustrations © 1997 by Bert Dodson
All rights reserved
Marshall Cavendish, 99 White Plains Road, Tarrytown, New York 10591
The text of this book is set in 14 point Veljovic Medium • The illustrations are rendered in watercolors • Printed in Italy
1 2 3 4 5 6 • First edition

Library of Congress Cataloging-in-Publication Data. Wittmann, Patricia. Buffalo thunder / Patricia Wittmann ;
illustrated by Bert Dodson.   p.   cm. Summary: When young Karl Isaac heads west with his family in a prairie
schooner, he experiences many things but longs to see buffalo. ISBN 0-7614-5001-7 (Reinforced binding)
[1. American bison—Fiction. 2. Frontier and pioneer life—Fiction.] I. Dodson, Bert, ill. II. Title.
PZ7.W78446Bu 1997   [E]—dc21   96-54893 CIP AC

*T*omorrow our journey begins. Everything we have fits like a puzzle in our new prairie schooner.

Pa is looking for some land. Ma is looking for a home. Lily and Baby are too young to care.

I, Karl Isaac, am looking for the wild and fierce buffalo.

I have never been kissed so much. Grammie and
Grampie walked with us as far as the creek. I gave them
ginger kitten. Be good and come back someday,
my Grammie said.

These mornings are frosty. Our new oxen are slow, but they suit me fine. I have named them Old Fly, Prince, Ruby, Sal, Duke, and Dime. The wagon creaks a hundred different ways as it rolls along. Ma fills the churn with cream and by night the wagon has rattled it to butter.

I am getting used to: cornbread
                    beans
                    walking all day
                    sleeping on the ground
                    wet boots
                    and more beans

Pa says we should be thankful for what we have. I will be thankful when I see buffalo.

I saw a cow drown today. A wagon tipped as it crossed the river. The folks grabbed hold of what they could and swam ashore. One man swam with a chicken on his head.

When it was our turn to cross, I sang rhymes to Lily and Baby. I didn't let them know I was scared too.

For days and days it has rained like everything. We travel
from one mudhole to the next. Wagons get stuck and folks are
throwin' things out.

    I counted: two washstands

              one tent

              seven cookstoves

              one piano, with fancy mirrors

              two plows

              three rocking chairs

The rocker Grampie made us is tied fast to our wagon.
Ma says our new home will need it.

We have joined a wagon train and left the last town behind.
Now we camp in a great circle of wagons. There is visiting after
supper and some folks dance.

This prairie sky is big enough to hold all the stars.
The fiddle sings like a bird in the night.

Indians! Pa hustled me into the wagon with Lily and Baby, but I spied them through the canvas. They wore blankets and beads and not much else. Their ponies were loaded high with buffalo skins.

Ma gave them our cornbread, then they wanted tea and
sugar, too. Ma was shaking by the time they left.
An Indian pony would be fine to ride in a buffalo hunt.

Today we passed a grave. It was small and covered
with stones. Pa said that's to keep the wolves away.

Eliza Newell Smith—aged 4 yrs. 3 mos.

Lily and I picked a posy of flowers to lay on the stones.

Our Lily is not much older than poor Eliza.

Today the wind blew so wild, it nearly pushed us across the prairie. Tin pans and hats flew in the air. In all the dust, Pa looked like a ghost leading the oxen along.

When it died down, we had to hunt for the cow. She got loose and wandered three miles back.

For supper we ate more dust than bread.

On this wide old prairie there are buffalo trails and buffalo wallows, but no matter how hard I look, there is not a beast in sight.

I listen to the men talk of sending scouts out to hunt. They would never let me go along.

The closest I get to a buffalo is picking up bushels of dried chips for the cookfire. Pa jokes that you don't have to pepper beans cooked over buffalo chips.

Will they ever pass this way again?

We have been gone seven weeks now. Our slowpoking train creeps along, one wagon after another. In the hot afternoons, Pa falls asleep, and Ma and I walk the oxen along. The grass is so tall it tickles my chin.

Ma says we are halfway between home and nowhere. I am inclined to agree. Halfway is a lonesome place.

This day started like any other, until thunder rumbled in a clear blue sky.

A dark cloud spread on the edge of the prairie like coffee boiling over. When folks shouted *stampede!* I wasn't surprised. I knew it was buffalo right from the start.

Ma scooped up the babies and hid inside the wagon. I stayed up top with Pa. I could feel buffalo coming through the bottoms of my feet.

The dust cloud got bigger. The wagon
shook and pans rattled, *rink-a-tink-a-tink*.
"Heaven help us," Pa said under his breath.

And then the buffalo were on us. They came so close, I was sure we'd be dashed to bits. Bellowing and snorting, they galloped with their beards to the ground and their tails in the air. Their hooves made a roar that ached in my ears.

More than I could ever count, more than I could even see, buffalo rushed by like a raging brown river. They kicked up a dust cloud that turned the wagons from white to gray.

When the wild rush finally came to an end, Ma's face was as gray as her apron. Baby was squallin' and Lily wouldn't come out.

Pa said he'll be glad to leave this prairie behind.
I tossed my hat high into the dusty air.
Yip-yip, YA-HOO!
It was the rip roarin'est time I have ever seen.

Today the prairie sun is hotter than ever. All that is left of yesterday is a mile wide trail of beaten-down grass.

But I, Karl Isaac, have seen the buffalo thunder.

Now, I am ready to look for our new home.